ROB THE ROMAN

Gets eaten by a Lion (nearly)

SCOULAR ANDERSON

■ SCHOLASTIC

For Jennifer

Scholastic Children's Books,
Commonwealth House, 1-19 New Oxford Street,
London WC1A 1NU, UK

A division of Scholastic Ltd
London ~ New York ~ Toronto ~ Sydney ~ Auckland
Mexico City ~ New Delhi ~ Hong Kong

Published in the UK by Scholastic Ltd, 2001

Text and Illustrations copyright © Scoular Anderson, 2001

ISBN 0 439 99253 2

CONTENTS

It was my turn to go for water.

But I didn't really mind going to the fountain. There's always much to see in the street.

Note for the future:
When I grow up, and I'm a rich, famous
gladiator, I'm going to have a house with 50
rooms (in the country, like grandpa). That's
46 more than we've got at the moment.

I got down to Via Squalida.
You have to keep glancing up when you're in the street – people are always emptying their piss pots out of the windows.

Wheels are banned during the day. Just imagine the traffic jams if they weren't.

I always get told off for taking too long to fetch water. Well, I can't help it if there are so many things to look at in the Via Squalida!

Note for the future:
When I grow up and I'm a rich, famous gladiator, I'm going to buy a pair of boots! Or even two pairs of boots!

I looked in at the barber's on the corner. Now, the barber's shop is always filled with people – not just having a shave but catching up with the gossip. It's a favourite meeting place.

I stood there for ages, watching and listening.

*Note for the future:
When I'm a rich, famous gladiator, I won't let anyone shave me. I'll grow a beard like the countrymen. And then they won't be able to stick my wounds up with spiders' webs, oil and vinegar either!*

Then the man being shaved turned round. It was my school teacher, Callidopolis!

I didn't want to feel Callidopolis's cane on my knuckles, so I ran all the way to the fountain!

The public loo is another great place for gossip.

Back home I got into trouble for being slow with the water.

Normally, we kids are taken to school by a slave. My dad's not very rich so we only have one slave – old Fustia. She doesn't know a wax tablet from a slice of cheese, but she's more like a granny than a slave. So, I usually go to school with Gratia and her slave, Fidelius.

OLD FUSTIA

FIDELIUS
HE MOANS A LOT

GRATIA

OUR PAL HILARIUS

ME - RUNNING LATE AS USUAL

Greetings, children!

PONG

WE MET OLD MA AUSPICIA COMING BACK FROM THE SHOPS WITH AN ANCIENT FISH. SHE'LL SPEND THE REST OF THE DAY PRODDING ITS GUTS AND COUNTING ITS BONES. THEN SHE'LL TELL US THAT THE EMPEROR WILL CATCH A COLD OR I'LL MEET TROUBLE WITH A CAT – STUPIDUS!

Callidopolis rents a little space from the baker to hold his school. The canvas screens give us a little privacy but they don't stop the noise. Callidopolis teaches us reading, writing and sums.

ALBINUS ALWAYS MISSES THE CHAMBERPOT

(I) LOVELY SMELL OF BREAD FROM THE BAKERY-SPLENDIDVS!

(II) MR CALLIDOPOLIS IS A GREEK. HE WAS ONCE A SLAVE BUT NOW HE IS A FREED MAN. GRANDPA SAYS THE BEST TEACHERS ARE GREEK BECAUSE THEY KNOW LOTS.

(III) ME TELLING GRATIA AND HILARIVS THAT ARGENTEVS AURIGA IS RACING NEXT DAY.
(IV) HILARIVS TELLING

ME AND GRATIA THAT HIS BIG BROTHER'S MATE IS A GUARD AT THE

Note for the future:
When I grow up and I'm a rich, famous gladiator, I'm going to have lots of paper and ink and pens to write and draw with. Callidopolis says it's too expensive for the likes of us.

BLUES' STABLE AND HE'LL GET US IN, NO PROBLEM. CAN'T WAIT!
Ⓥ MR VINARIUS THE WINE-SELLER LIKES TO TASTE ALL HIS WINE BEFORE HE SELLS IT.
Ⓥ MR MEDICUS. HE USED TO BE A SLAVE, TOO, THEN HE WAS MADE A FREED MAN. FIRSTLY, HE WORKED AS AN UNDERTAKER, NOW HE'S A DOCTOR. FOUR SLAVES CARRY HIS MEDICINE BOXES. DAD SAYS HE'D RATHER EAT A MOUTHFUL OF MUD FROM THE RIVER THAN TRY ONE OF MEDICUS'S POTIONS!

CHARIOTS·AND·CHEERS

Next morning, Mum said it was my turn to get the water again. It was really my sister's turn. Where was she?

She's gone out.

What? At this time of the morning?

There was a great crowd at the barber's. What was going on? Even my sister was there. I asked her if she was in the queue for a shave.

I managed to push my way to the front. On the barber's stool was Argenteus Auriga, the charioteer! They say he is so rich that he owns a villa in the country.

I only got a short look because he soon swept out, surrounded by his bodyguards. Charioteers are OK, but they're not as splendid as gladiators.

In the afternoon, Gratia, Hilarius and me headed for the Circus where the races are held. Fidelius came too, though he moaned like the clappers.

(I) THERE ARE PICTURES OF THE TOP CHARIOTEERS STUCK UP EVERYWHERE.

(II) MR THERMOPOLIUM'S SNACK BAR DOES A ROARING TRADE ON RACE DAYS SELLING SNACKS AND DRINKS TO THE FANS.

(III) ALEAS IS SELLING RAFFLE TICKETS FROM HIS FAVOURITE PITCH OUTSIDE THE SNACK BAR.

The streets were crammed with fans. You could see team colours everywhere. The Blues (yesss!), the Reds, the Whites, and the Greens.

IV HILARIUS SAYS HIS BIG BROTHER INEPTUS MADE A CURSE TABLET LAST RACE DAY. HE SCRATCHED 'I HOPE AMPLIATUS WILL CRASH HIS CHARIOT,' ON A BIT OF POTTERY AND BURIED IT IN A SPECIAL PLACE. AMPLIATUS WON. SO MUCH FOR CURSES!

V MONUMENTUS SELLS RACE SOUVENIRS IN THE ARCADE. YOU CAN BUY POTS WITH FAMOUS HORSE'S NAMES ON THEM.

We got caught up between two lots of fans.

They often started fighting.

We got to the Blues' stable and Hilarius's brother sneaked us in by a back door. The place was heaving with people.

There were stable boys, grooms, saddlers, waterers, horse surgeons and the rich men who put up the money. Then Argenteus Auriga arrived.

We watched him being prepared. He had his eyes shut – calming himself before the race.

WHIP

HELMET

TUNIC IN TEAM COLOURS

PROTECTIVE WAISTCOAT

KNIFE (HORSE REINS WILL BE TIED ROUND HIS WAIST TO LEAVE HIS HANDS FREE. IF THERE IS A CRASH, HE WILL CUT THE REINS FREE WITH THE KNIFE.)

PROTECTIVE LEGGINGS

The horses were ready for the parade. They had wreathes on their heads and pearls on their manes. Their tails were tied in neat knots and their collars were decorated with good-luck trinkets and ribbons in the team colours.

But the pre-race parade was about to begin, with lots of loud music, dancers and acrobats! *Splendidus, Splendidissimus!*

The chariotcers were there, and some priests wafting incense about.

We got seats in front of two old blokes. They'd brought cushions to sit on.

We had a brilliant view.

There was cheering. The magistrate came up onto the balcony. (A fat guy who's a councillor, or something. He was wearing a golden crown that was so heavy his slaves had to hold it upright for him!)

He raised a hand with a napkin in it. He dropped the napkin. THEY WERE OFF!

The old guys beside us were giving a running commentary!

IV STATUE OF CONSUS, THE GOD OF THE CIRCUS.	V THE BIT DOWN THE MIDDLE IS CALLED THE SPINA.	VI MARBLE SEATS FOR POSH FOLK. VII WOODEN SEATS. VIII STANDING ROOM ONLY.	IX AURIGA WILL HAVE TO USE ALL HIS SKILLS TO GET AHEAD.	X THE CIRCUS IS A GOOD PLACE TO TO SIT BESIDE YOUR GIRLFRIEND. (SO HILARIUS'S BROTHER SAYS)

Argenteus Auriga was the winner again!
Splendidus! Splendidissimus

Note for the future:
If I don't become a rich, famous gladiator, I might become a rich, famous charioteer instead.

MUSIC AND MEATBALLS

Who was sitting in the barber's next morning? It was cousin Ossius. He was having his first shave. Good luck to him! No wonder he looked worried.

The barber spat on his whetstone and sharpened his knife.

Uncle Pomposius and Aunt Gloriosa were there, too.

The first shave is an important ceremony. Ossius, the boy, was about to become Ossius, the man. Uncle and Aunt were holding a party to celebrate and we were invited.

Now Uncle Pomposius is very rich and he doesn't speak much to us, as my dad is just a poor Inspector of Drains. This was the first time I'd seen inside Uncle's house. I was allowed to go early and play with Gratia.

Can you believe it! Uncle even sent two big slaves with a carrying-chair to collect me.

When I arrived, Gratia and I played for a bit. She has lots of toys and board games. Then she took me round the house.

WOW! It was some place! It was huge and filled with fancy furniture. There were people everywhere. In one room there was a man making a new mosaic. That means he was pressing little bits of coloured stone onto wet plaster on the floor. It looked brilliant!

In another room, artists were painting beautiful pictures on the walls.

In the next room, there was a gate into a nice garden with a statue in it. Well, I thought it was a gate but Gratia explained it was just a trick painting that looked like a real gate. I found that out for myself when I tried to walk through it.

Then we went through the real gate into the real garden.

I. UNCLE KEEPS TREES AND HEDGES NEATLY CLIPPED.

II. AUNTIE'S FAVOURITE FLOWERS: ROSES, LILIES AND IRISES.

III. GRATIA SAYS THAT UNCLE SOMETIMES PUTS FOOD IN BOATS FOR GUESTS TO FISH OUT OF THE POND.

Gratia took me to the kitchen where the special meal was being prepared. Gratia says Uncle's chief cook, Flaccidus, gets into a terrible temper if things go wrong and he throws things around the kitchen. Some of them were still there.

37

Uncle Pomposius was working in his library with his secretary.

Aunt Gloriosa was getting ready for the party. We sneaked into a doorway and watched. I realized that Auntie has hardly any hair!!

Nearby, there was a table full of pots of stuff to make Auntie beautiful.

A slave came and put a mixture of powdered chalk and white lead on Auntie's arms and face to make her look pale and delicate.

AUNTIE HAD RED OCHRE (A SORT OF MASHED UP CLAY - YUK!) PUT ON HER LIPS.

SHE HAD BLACK ASHES PUT ON HER EYELASHES AND ROUND HER EYES.

HER CHEEKS WERE ROUGED WITH WINE DREGS.

HER TEETH WERE POLISHED WITH POWDERED ANIMAL HORN.

LILIA PUT A WIG ON AUNTIE'S HEAD. IT WAS MADE FROM THE HAIR OF SLAVES.

BLONDE HAIR IS VERY FASHIONABLE.

EARRINGS OF PEARL AND GREEN STONES WENT ON HER EARS.

FINE GOLD CHAINS WENT ROUND HER NECK.

BANGLES IN THE SHAPE OF

SNAKES WENT ROUND HER WRISTS. THEY ARE SAID TO BRING LONG LIFE!

GOLD RINGS SET

WITH GEMS FOR HER FINGERS.

SHE PUT CIRCLETS OF GOLD ON HER ANKLES.

SHE WAS DRESSED IN CLOTH OF THE MOST BRILLIANT COLOURS.

IN ONE HAND SHE HELD A NAPKIN TO DAB THE SWEAT FROM HER FACE.

IN THE OTHER HAND SHE HELD A FAN OF PEACOCK FEATHERS TO SWAT FLIES.

AUNTIE WAS READY FOR THE PARTY!

For the dinner, the grown-ups lay on couches as usual. Since Ossius was now grown-up he lay on a couch, too. We kids sat on stools.

Auntie's little dog, Cupidus, sat under the table hoping for scraps. But the mosaic pattern on the dining room floor showed pictures of scraps like chicken bones and pips and things. This was one of Uncle's jokes but it didn't half confuse Cupidus.

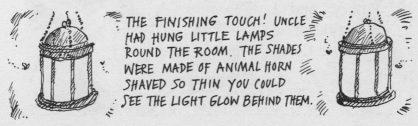

THE FINISHING TOUCH! UNCLE HAD HUNG LITTLE LAMPS ROUND THE ROOM. THE SHADES WERE MADE OF ANIMAL HORN SHAVED SO THIN YOU COULD SEE THE LIGHT GLOW BEHIND THEM.

The food was never ending! There were more of Uncle's jokes. For instance, the slaves brought in a huge wooden hen and we had to search the straw underneath to find boiled eggs!

Uncle had laid on entertainment while we ate. There was a poet who read some of his poems.
There was a lottery, and I won first prize – a little flute!

There were some musicians and dancers from Egypt.

The grown-ups became very merry because they drank a lot of wine. Uncle sang a song and Auntie's wig fell into the pudding (which was a model of the Amphitheatre, made of sweet stuff and full of spiced fruit).

Note for the future:
I'm not looking forward to my first shave, but if I'm going to be a gladiator I have to be brave. I'll look forward to the party afterwards, though. I'm going to have hundreds of musicians.

FALSE TEETH AND FREEDOM

I went downstairs to fetch water. Yes, me again! I met old Ma Auspicia and, as usual, she was holding something disgusting in her hand.

Someone called to me from the barber's. At first, I didn't recognize him.

Grandpa rummaged in his bag. He pulled something out and put it in his mouth. Then he gave a big smile.

He was in the city to do a little business. Dad had persuaded him to take me to his farm for a short stay – to see if I would like farming. (Dad doesn't want me to be a gladiator.) Mum was worried about the highwaymen who attack travellers. Grandpa said his big slave, Molussus, could scare off 20 bandits.

The main road out of the city was very exciting. Traffic everywhere! There were carts carrying logs, or cabbages, or hunks of marble, or passengers.

I GRANDPA TOLD ME TO COUNT THE MILESTONES WE PASSED. HE SAID EACH MILE WAS A THOUSAND PACES. THEN I COULD CALCULATE HOW MANY STEPS OUR JOURNEY HAD TAKEN.

II I GET ENOUGH SUMS FROM CALLIDOPOLIS! ANYWAY, IT'S NOT US THAT'S PACING, IT'S THE MULE. I WONDER IF MULE PACES ARE DIFFERENT FROM OURS?

There were fast chariots carrying important government mail. There were companies of soldiers on the march and gangs of slaves mending the road.

We used a fantastic bridge to cross a deep valley. It was so high it was quite scary to look down!

We stopped at a tavern for some lunch. It wasn't very good. The bread and cheese was stale and the water tasted funny. Grandpa said roadside taverns are often like this.

Then we took a shortcut through the marshes on the canal. We hired a boat, but only after Grandpa had argued a lot about the fare. He said it was too expensive. Some slaves working nearby joined in the argument and I thought there was going to be a fight.

The mule pulling the barge was about 100 years old and very slow. The place was filled with noisy frogs and biting mosquitoes.

At last we reached Grandpa's big villa and his farm. We stopped at a shrine by the gate. Grandpa rummaged in his bag and found his false teeth. He looked again and found some little biscuits. He laid them on the shrine as an offering to the gods. Then he said a prayer.

Oh godsh, I give thanksh for our shafe journey, free from muggersh. Pleashe continue to protect my farm and family.

Oh, praise to Juno and Fortuna that you have returned safely!

For the next few days I helped out on the farm.

I helped to carry the animal muck out to the fields – yuk!

Grapes were being brought in from the vineyards. I watched them being trampled to squeeze the juice out. I had a go myself.

The grape pulp that was left was squeezed even more in a huge machine in a huge shed. I had a go at that, too.

After that I helped pour the juice into big pots sunk into the ground in the courtyard. The grape juice is left there to turn into wine. Phew!

Finally, I had to go and clean myself up, ready for a special ceremony. Grandpa was going to free his faithful slave and companion, Molussus. A very important man came from the town to be a witness. He gave Molussus a special cap to wear and touched him with a stick.

Grandpa and Molussus hugged each other and shed a tear. Molussus would still work for Grandpa, but he could leave if he wanted to.

Molussus's first task was to take me back home to the city, along with a load of hay. I was exhausted!

BY THIS TIME, GRANDPA HAD THROWN OFF HIS TOGA WHICH HE CALLED A HORRID, HOT, PRICKLY THING. HE HAD TOSSED HIS WIG INTO THE COMPOST HEAP AND PUT HIS SPECIAL TEETH AWAY IN A CUPBOARD.

AS FOR ME, PHEW!

Note for the Future:
When I'm a rich, famous gladiator, I'll have a place in the country, but I'll make sure I don't have to do any work!

SWEAT AND SWIMMING

There was great excitement in the Via Squalida the next morning! A fire started on the top floor of one of the buildings. The fire fighters arrived quickly.

They had to run up several flights of stairs with their buckets and sponges on long poles. (The sponges are to douse walls with water to stop the fire spreading.) Luckily, it wasn't a big fire.

Note for the future:
When I'm a rich,
famous gladiator, I
might help the fire
fighters. I'll be good
at running up
all those
stairs.

Talking of water, Ossius had promised to take me to the Public Baths. I think he really wanted to show me his weight-lifting technique. (He's got a weedy body!) He met me outside the barber's.

Now, I'd only been to our local bath house which is dark and smelly and so titchy that three people in the bath was a real crowd. Ossius says that the Public Baths are the biggest in the world.

There are lots of shops in the arcades outside the baths. Ossius bought some food – apples and pies.

Ossius is always stuffing his face. He says it helps to build up a fantastic body.

There were some quite posh shops selling everything you might need in the baths, like towels and perfumed oils and strigils. Ossius says strigils are for scraping the gunge off you.

Ossius had to pay as he is an adult. Kids get in free.

The baths are seriously big!

| THE BATHS ARE DECORATED WITH STATUES OF THE IMPORTANT GODS | Ⅰ THIS ONE IS JUPITER, KING OF THE GODS. | Ⅱ THIS ONE IS VENUS, GODDESS OF LOVE AND BEAUTY. | Ⅲ THIS ONE IS NEPTUNE, GOD OF THE SEA. I THINK HE IS MY FAVOURITE GOD. | Ⅳ THE WALLS AND CEILING ARE COVERED IN PICTURES OF SEA CREATURES. |

Ⅴ) A LOAD OF OLD FAT GUYS SITTING AROUND. OSSIUS SAYS THE BATHS ARE A SORT OF CLUB WHERE PEOPLE COME TO MEET.

Ⅵ) AN UGLY GREAT PIG SLIPPED AND FELL AND I LAUGHED. THAT WAS THE WRONG THING TO DO. OOPS.

Ⅶ) WHILE I WAS LOOKING AT THE UGLY PIG, I KNOCKED A JAR OF OIL FROM SOMEONE'S HAND - MORE PEOPLE ON THE FLOOR. TIME TO EXIT!

61

We went into the changing room and took off our clothes. Ossius slipped a few coins to a slave to keep an eye on our things, otherwise they might have disappeared by the time we got back.

Ossius said we had to follow a routine. First of all, we had to work up a sweat in the exercise yard. There were lots of men and women there, grunting and groaning.

I watched the wrestlers! They slapped oil and wax all over their bodies to keep their skin supple, then they covered themselves in dust so they could get a grip on each other.

And I saw a man who was so lazy, he got his slave to pick up the ball every time he missed a catch!

THEY'RE PLAYING TRIGON, A BALL-THROWING GAME FOR THREE PLAYERS ON A TRIANGULAR PITCH.

I went and played with some other kids who were kicking and throwing a ball around. The Ugly Great Pig I laughed at was there and he gave me aggro. Ossius had to come and rescue me.

A bell rang to tell us that the baths were open. At the entrance there was a mosaic on the floor which said:

We went into the Calidarium, which is a really hot and steamy room. Phew! People were being massaged in there.

(I) OSSIUS SAYS THE SWEAT REMOVES MUCK FROM YOUR BODY. I'LL HAVE NOTHING LEFT IN MY BODY AFTER THIS!

(II) I'M TRYING NOT TO MOVE BECAUSE THE WATER IS SO HOT.

(III) OF COURSE, WHEN I'M A RICH AND FAMOUS GLADIATOR, I'LL HAVE ONE OF THESE PRIVATE BOXES TO BATHE IN.

Next, we went into the Tepidarium which was not too hot and not too cold. I almost went to sleep!

Then we plunged into the pool in the Frigidarium. This was really COLD and a bit of a shock.

I caught sight of the old guys who sat beside us at the races. They were still nattering.

We headed for the exit but we saw the Ugly Great Pig waiting for us. Luckily, Ossius knew a back way out. We went through lots of doors and passageways.

If you think the hot baths are hot, you should feel the heat in the boiler room! There are huge furnaces blazing away in there to heat the water.

Hot air flows under the floor and behind the walls. I know because I saw some men repairing a duct under the floor.

The furnaces need forests of wood! The baths need lakes of water! There is a huge aqueduct that brings water from far away right into the baths.

Got home safely, without being thumped again by the Ugly Great Pig.

SHIPS ·AND· SLAVES

Well, who was sitting in the barber's chair the next morning? It was ME! I was glad I was looking out into the street and not at the barber's awful scissors. Don't worry, I wasn't in for a shave.

Note for the future: When I'm a rich, famous gladiator, I'll have crowds of fans watching my hair cuts through the window.

It was part of a bargain. Dad said I looked scruffy and he would take me to the port to see the ships if I got a haircut.

THIS IS THE CART THAT DAD HAD HIRED TO TAKE US TO THE PORT →

← THE CARTER'S DOG

Gratia and her minder, Fidelius, came to the port with us. Dad's secretary came, too. Then there were two slaves who came to lift the drain covers when Dad wanted to inspect something. It was a bit of a squash.

FUG

ONE OF THE SLAVES HAD 'FUG' (SHORT FOR FUGITIVE) TATOOED ON HIS BROW. THAT MEANT HE HAD TRIED TO RUN AWAY ONCE.

THE OTHER SLAVE.

DAD'S SECRETARY, SCRIBUS.

DAD

FIDELIUS- LOOKING AS CHEERFUL AS EVER.

ME AND GRATIA AT THE BACK WE HAD A GOOD VIEW.

Note for the future:
When I'm a rich, famous gladiator, I'll get
a chariot with springy wheels so it doesn't
jolt about so much. I told Dad that but he
wasn't impressed.

Just as we left the gates of the city there was a
wild noise up ahead. Dad said it was a funeral
procession.
First, we passed the dead person's relatives at
the end of the procession.

Then we passed the professional mourners who were paid to weep and wail.

Then we came to the dead person who was lying on a couch, just as if he was having a good sleep. Dad said he'd have a coin under his tongue to pay the ghostly ferryman who would row him over the river to the Underworld.

At the very front of the procession were the musicians. What a racket! Dad said the dead man must have been very important.

Our cart pushed on and we passed the tombs of other very important people that line the road out of the city.

We got to the port. It is a busy place! Stuff arrives here from all over the Empire.

The streets are lined with warehouses. You can tell who owns them because there are signs outside on the pavement.

There were slaves being taken off a ship and up to the slave market. There were men, women and children. Dad said that some slaves will have a hard life – like working down the mines or as an oarsman in a warship. Others will become doctors or teachers.

Dad went off to inspect a load of pipes for some new drains. He told us to wait where we were until he came back. Well, that was boring! Gratia and me went off exploring...

...and had a close encounter with a lion.

The slaves who were moving the cage had a good laugh. They told us the lion had just come from Africa and was off to the games at the Amphitheatre.

Note for the future:
I didn't know lions were as big as that. When I'm a rich, famous gladiator, I'll try not to do too much fighting.

Dad came back with a present for each of us – pocket knives! Mine was in the shape of a dog, Gratia's was a dolphin.

Just before we set off for home, we saw a warship pass beyond the lighthouse.

TRAINING ·AND· TACTICS

Next day, I slipped out of the house before I was asked to go for water. I heard Mum calling me so I didn't stop at the barber's but hurried down the lane.

Then I heard another shout behind me. Someone had just leapt out of the barber's. He still had the barber's cloth around his shoulders.

Illustrius was home on leave from the army. We went into a nearby snack bar so he could tell me all about it.

I. TONSORIUS COMING TO FIND HIS BARBER'S CLOTH.

II. PICTORIUS THE PAINTER'S PRIZE FIGHTING COCK. PICTORIUS IS CELEBRATING HIS WIN OF THREE FIGHTS. GAMBLING IS THE FAVOURITE ROMAN PASTIME SO...

III. IN FIVE MINUTES PICTORIUS IS GOING TO LOSE ALL HIS WINNINGS WHEN HE GAMBLES ON A GAME OF DICE.

We did a lot of square-bashing – learning to march...

...at military pace with short, quick steps...

...or at full pace – that's long strides for route marches.

We've done weapons-training with wooden swords against a wooden pole...

I

...the secret is to keep the hilt of the sword low and use stabbing motions to the head, lower body or legs.

push off if you're going to play games!

III

II

I BARMAID WONDERING WHERE HER SPOON HAS GONE.

II DICE-PLAYER GETTING PUT OFF BY THE FIGHTING DEMONSTRATION.

III ME IMAGINING WHAT IT WOULD BE LIKE FOR REAL.

85

Illustrius seemed to be enjoying himself in the army. He said he would like to get posted to Britain where he could see the giant wall that the Emperor Hadrian has built there. Then Illustrius rummaged in his bag and brought out two tokens.

My mum doesn't approve of what goes on at the Amphitheatre, but I was desperate to see a gladiator in action at last.

The Amphitheatre is a huge place with thousands of seats. Sometimes they fill the arena with water and hold mock sea battles.

When we got inside, Illustrius said he was
going to get us some food. He told me to make
my way up to the seats.

I must have taken
a wrong turning
somewhere. I found
myself going down
rather than up.

Soon, I was in a great maze of dark corridors.
They echoed with the noise of wild animals. I
turned a corner and...

...thought I was going to get eaten alive!

But worse was to come! I bumped into some of the slaves who work down there.

They pushed me
into a cage.

They hoisted the cage upwards through the darkness. Then the door clanged open and I could see a ramp ahead.

The only way I could go was up.

The trap-door at the top suddenly swung open.
This time there was no escape. I really was
going to be eaten alive!

I was in the middle of the Amphitheatre arena.
There were lions, tigers, elephants. They were
huge, they were terrifying, and they were all …

TAME! *Splendidus, splendidissimus!* This wasn't the fight, it was the big parade that opens the games. What a stroke of luck!

I joined the parade. I hoped no one would notice me. The animals did clever tricks. The orchestra played. The crowd cheered.

Then the gladiators arrived in chariots. They stepped down, followed by slaves holding their weapons. They all saluted the Emperor.

The weapons were inspected and the blunt ones were taken away. The gladiators looked terrifying. They spat, and swore and played with their weapons. They were mostly slaves or criminals who had been trained at a gladiator school.

I know I fancied being a gladiator but this was a bit too close for comfort. I was having second thoughts.

The gladiators began to fight. Their trainers shouted instructions at them.

When I saw the first blood I felt a little queasy. One wounded gladiator fell down. The winning gladiator turned to the crowd to find out if they wanted him finished off.

But the spectators thought he had fought well. They gave him the thumbs up. The Emperor then gave the thumbs up sign, too. The gladiator was saved.

When slaves came into the arena to pick up the bodies of the dead gladiators, I saw my chance to escape and followed them. Just in time, too. The wild beasts were about to enter the arena!

And there was Illustrius! He had come down to try and rescue me. I was quite glad to let him take me home.

And did Robur become a gladiator or a barber or a Inspector of Drains like his dad?

HERE LIE THE BONES OF ROBUR THE ROMAN, THE MOST FAMOUS DESIGNER OF DRAINS IN THE EMPIRE. IN OLD AGE HE WAS ONCE FRIGHTENED BY A CAT WHICH MADE HIM FALL INTO ONE OF HIS OWN DRAINS AND HE WAS FLUSHED INTO THE SEA (NEARLY).